SONG OF DUISKE

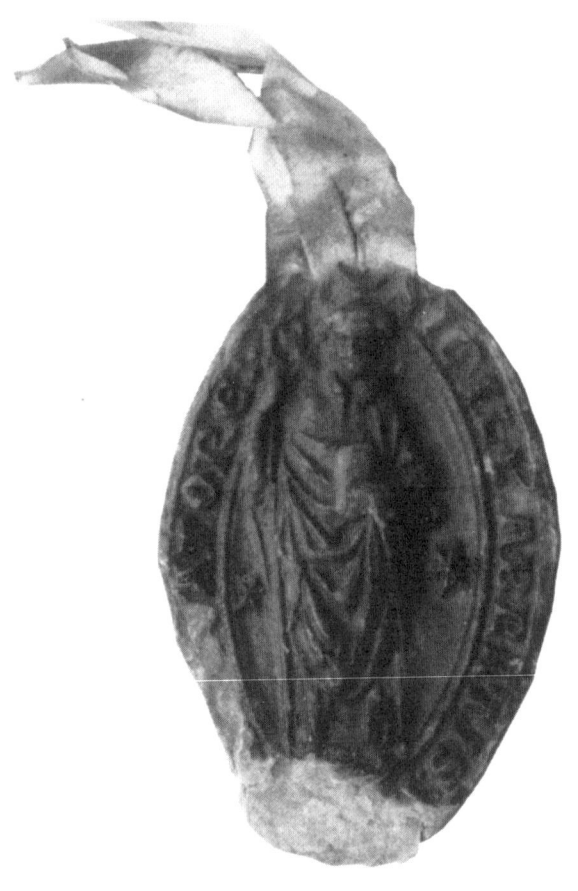

Seal of Duiske Abbey

John A. Ryan

SONG OF DUISKE

THE LILLIPUT PRESS

Copyright © John A. Ryan 1989, 2006

All rights reserved. No part of this publication may be reproduced in any form or by any means without the prior permission of the publisher.

First published in 1989, revised 2006 by
THE LILLIPUT PRESS LTD
62-63 Sitric Road, Arbour Hill,
Dublin 7, Ireland
www.lilliputpress.ie

British Library Cataloguing in Publication Data

Ryan, John A. (John Aloysius), *1923* –
Song of Duiske
I. Title
823'.914 [f]

ISBN 0 946640 37 8
ISBN 978 0 946640 37 9

Set in 11 on 13 Garamond by Redsetter Ltd
and printed by Betaprint of Dublin

CONTENTS

Illustrations and Acknowledgments vi
Historical Notes vii
Dramatis Personae viii
Map ix

I Dark 1
II Seed 7
III Earth 23
IV Harvest 31
V Home 45

Glossary 53

Illustrations and Acknowledgments

The ship depicted on the map on p. ix is the common medieval cargo ship called a cog. This drawing is based on a seal of the Baltic port of Stralsund, dated 1329

The frontispiece shows a late thirteenth-century seal of Duiske Abbey affixed to a charter now in the National Library of Ireland. It depicts the standing figure of an abbot holding a book and crozier. The inscription reads 'SIGILL ABBATIS DE [SALV]ATORE'. (Photograph courtesy of Roger Stalley.)

The decorated initial letters on pp. 3, 9, 25, 33 and 47 are taken from a manuscript of the Epistles of St Gregory which once belonged to Duiske Abbey and is now in the British Library, London. (Re-drawn courtesy of Frank Gaule.)

The publisher would like to thank John Bradley, Director of the Urban Archaeology Survey, for his professional advice and interest in the work.

HISTORICAL NOTE

The great Cistercian abbeys of Ireland were built between the years 1100 and 1300. Mellifont was the earliest and is probably the best known. Among the many kings and chieftains who founded abbeys in their territories was Dermot Mac Murrough, King of Leinster, who founded Baltinglass. His vassal, Diarmaid Ó Riain of Uí Dróna, founded Killenny, or *Vallis Dei*, near the present-day Goresbridge, and gave land for another abbey about six miles farther south where the little river Duiske flows into the Barrow and where the town of Graiguenamanagh now stands. Both sites were on the western bank of the Barrow in County Kilkenny, which may indicate that Uí Dróna was at that time more extensive than the present baronies of Idrone East and Idrone West in County Carlow. Plans for the founding of the second abbey were disrupted by the Norman invasion of 1169.

County Kilkenny was acquired by William Marshal, Earl of Pembroke, and it was he who renewed Ó Riain's grant of land and founded the abbey of Duiske, or *Vallis Sancti Salvatoris*. The first community came from Stanley in Wiltshire, and Duiske remained very Norman, in personnel and in spirit, compared with other abbeys such as Killenny or Killenny's mother-house Jerpoint, ten miles away to the west near the river Nore.

There was further cause for bad feeling between Duiske and Jerpoint: when Killenny was reduced to the status of a grange by the Cistercian General Chapter of 1227, it was put under the control of Duiske, and, Jerpoint naturally resenting this, a long feud followed between the two abbeys.

Song of Duiske, then, takes place in the year 1304, one hundred years after the foundation of the abbey. At that time it was doing a brisk trade in wool with the merchants of Lucca in Tuscany, in return importing wine, glassware, iron, fruit and textiles. The narrative stays reasonably close to the historical and geographical facts but makes no claim to strict accuracy.

Dramatis Personae

Brother Simon: there is some disagreement as to his place of birth, some maintaining that he was born in Ireland in 1254, others that he was born in England *circa* 1246 and was sent to Ireland from the abbey of Stanley. He became Cellarer in 1295 when Duiske was already in debt to the merchants of Lucca. He lived to a great age and is said to have been taken at length by the Black Death. No stone marks his grave in the Abbey's burial ground.

Brother Orion: little is known of him. It is thought he may have been a natural son of Ó Maolriain of Uí Dróna, descendant of that same Diarmaid Ó Riain who founded Killenny. Ó Maolriain was now, in 1304, much reduced in power and territory, if perhaps not in pride.

The Earl: Gilbert de Clare, Earl of Hertford and Gloucester, Lord of the Liberties of Kilkenny. He was killed fighting for his king at Bannockburn in the year 1314. He was the last of his name.

I
DARK

WHILE the voice of the bell still hung on the shivering air Brother Simon was out of bed, feet wincing from the cold of the smooth stone floor. Quickly he crossed the dormitory where vague ghosts rustled all around him. He reached the arched stairhead, was first down the nightstair, glimpsed through a slitted window high in the stone a merciless black sky and one glittering star. Now the chill silence of the morning denied that a bell had lately called or ever could have called, but it rang still in Simon's thought. He put his hands into his wide sleeves and stepped down. A candle-flame shook, shadows danced, and Brother Porter was only one sconce ahead, breathing heavily, working feverishly with his taper and as always leaving half unlighted.

'Lord, Lord, forbearance give to me that I may not notice incompetent blunderers.'

From his place he saw the dim hooded shapes flit by. No face, no hands, a shuffle of sandals on the worn tiles.

The monks' choir was not so decorous; a great flurry of noise as three of the choir-monks pushed, pulled, lifted old Father Gout into position.

At last, silence.

Now you could hear the stones whisper. The massive pillars stood strong and proud; the stone ribs curved up and up and up into the blackness. Candle-flames twitched nervously. Frost curled toes and pulled cowls closer.

From far off came the Abbot's voice. The other voices followed. Up soared the pointed Latin, swelled until it filled all those sombre shadows among the arches. It silenced the squeaking stones, threw back shoulders and cowls.

There came a tremendous clatter and commotion from the dim reaches of the choir. Old Father Gout had fallen out of his stall again. Simon's thoughts wavered from his prayer – a pity about the Abbot's singing, his Latin tainted with French, his tenor with falsetto. Were it not for Brother Cantor that tenor would rise until it disappeared into the massy vaults and joined the throng of stars in the night sky. The Brethren, however, thought the Abbot's pronunciation so distinguished, his tenor so devotional.

'Lord, grant me charity, that I may not know a good singer from a bad.'

Brother Orion pondered the advantages of being a Cistercian lay-brother. There was fine singing all around him, but it was not only that, but many other things. Oh indeed winters were cold, but summers, ah, summers were warm. And autumn cornfields lit by a harvest moon. *Iam Lucis*. There were privileges, too: Pontage, Lastage, Stallage, Portage, Wastage, Ullage – what a litany; Knockage, Loppage and Cleavage, the Abbey enjoyed all of these and more. Cleavage was best. It warmed him in dim and dark when frost shivered the stones and a man's hand stuck to the iron bolt when he went to open it at glittering dawn-time, and the red sun peered angrily through bare branches, and then to think of Cleavage. It warmed so many times. The forest had great shelter, a man could be happy there all day with a fine axe, soft moss and wood-flakes underfoot. Split a log from the head. The kitchens then, warmest place of all, with logs roaring out their heat, or the bakehouse, when you bore in armfuls of timber and piled it near the ovens. The calefactory was but a place for cool scholars. The towering oaks by their life and by their death kept life in men when the sun failed them. The Rule – ah yes, there was the Rule. It could be – interpreted. *Exempli gratia*: No female foot shall tread the Abbey stair. Vespers, midnight, cock-crow, dawn. He considered that in general it was a good Rule – there are many ways out of a cornfield, only one way down a stair.

Matins were ending. Brother Orion joined enthusiastically in the singing of the last line. He never failed to give thanks for his good fortune.

It was Brother Timothy's turn at the great mill. He was trustworthy, enthusiastic and inexperienced. Early, early, while the stars still showed, he went up the mill stair to begin the day's work. It was soon clear that something was wrong: his wheel did not turn, he could not understand why. There should have been abundant power all through the winter when Duiske came down heavy with flood-water. He went out again into the wan light and mounted the revetment.

The mill-race came towards him, full, threatening, its edges touched with ice. It fell thunderously over the spillway in black and silver. It did not turn his wheel; an alder bough had fallen to block the race, flotsam of sticks and grasses, ice in thin curving ledges. Something else also was amiss; part of the embankment had broken and the escaping water made a spongy morass of the slope where it found its way down to Duiske again. Young and strong, he did not go for help. He went to the mill and returned with an axe, a shovel, a rope, and, working quickly but very carefully because there was little light, he made a temporary repair with branches and earth. Then, having tied his rope to the fallen alder, he looped it round a strong sapling that grew on the bank and pulled steadily. One thing he had forgotten – all was still in mesh, and so when the alder came slowly out half onto the bank and the eager water was released, his wheel ran wild. At once he knew his mistake. He rushed in panic down the revetment, slipped on the icy slope, his sopping habit impeding him, and fell headlong, his hands so numb that he hardly noticed them cut on the iron-hard ground, then scrambling to his feet again he flew up the stairs and threw over the lever. The racing wheels came to a stop but the damage was done. Years of grinding work had worn the nether stone to the condition where the added strain was too much. It cracked across.

Brother Timothy, out of breath, his hands beginning to feel their hurt through the bitter cold of the water, his wet habit clinging to his knees, his feet gone, gone, where were they? he could not feel them – he fell to his knees, leaned his head on the stone, and sobbed.

Brother Simon and Brother Shepherd parted just beyond the gate, Shepherd to climb the steep path that would bring him to the sheep-fold, Simon to march briskly along the *Via Magna*. The spangled heaven lit the way with a faint silver. Simon pulled his cloak tight. The broad path, hard as rock, black with cold, gleamed here and there in ice-puddles, and he could see the hurrying stream with its grey-rimed alders. A star danced in the brimming water of the race. Five hundred paces brought him to where the bridge crossed to the mill. There all was still and idle, and mounting the stairs he found Timothy kneeling on the floor in the flour-dust licking the blood and tears from his knuckles. He looked up with sad eyes and pointed to the riven stone, so Simon knelt beside him and they prayed together and Simon added silently, 'Patience, Lord, give to me, for not everyone is as careful and far-seeing as I.'

Through the eastern window he saw the low red sun that now at last deigned to peer down from the shoulder of Blackstair on his deserted world, where waters thickened, the brittle leaf shivered and the trees smoked with frost.

II
SEED

COMING from the eel-weirs, Brother Simon reached the grove of chestnut trees that gave their orchard shelter from the east. They had grown well but did not always ripen their fruit. Abbot John, God rest him, had wanted to cut them down and replace them with walnuts, but Brother Agapanthus had had doubts about that. The chestnuts were in no danger now from Abbot John, who slept nearby, untroubled by such things, and the years had shown that walnuts had just as little liking for the summers of Blackwater, cooler than their homeland. Agapanthus was working at the apple trees. He smiled at Brother Simon. Simon looked cold. Working, Agapanthus reflected, was warmer than over-seeing.

'Look at our medlars as you go down. Surely they will bear a crop this year.'

'Please God,' answered Simon.

He hurried away down the alleys of damson, medlar and quince. He tightened his cloak. The wind came from the east to search among the branches. It bundled leaves into corners where they stirred and whispered. Under the trees the spears of the cuckoo-pint were new; they had not yet come to their strength but seemed to be waiting. Catkins on the hazel-rods also waited. They had not loosened yet to spill their yellow gold. And winter hung on and would not let go. Only in a sheltered place near the church, butterbur showed in a scatter of pink. From the eastern gable the cold light was reflected in the three tall lancets.

Simon as Cellarer saw to the running of most of the Abbey's business activities; the Prior was not an active man and the keeping of accounts was more to his liking. It was not easy, however, to have a knowledge of all; in the matter of farm animals and of the woodlands Orion was Simon's choice of helper.

He found Brother Orion in the brewhouse. Their first call was to the great mill.

'Without our great mill we can do only half the grinding needed. We must replace our nether stone. I fear many small querns are in use in secret and this cannot be allowed.'

The thought that privileges might be usurped in such a way upset Simon; but Orion had seen more hand-querns in use than Simon had ever dreamed of.

'No indeed,' he murmured.

The fragments of the broken stone would have to be removed.

'Here the sheerlegs will squat. They should be eighteen or twenty measures in length,' said Orion, gauging with his eye.

'Thirty,' Simon said firmly, and, to Orion's lifted eyebrow, 'we may have other uses for them. Let us have them long enough.'

Orion's eyes filled bright with a thought.

'Brother, what better way to spend today than to go to choose our trees in Gorlough Wood.'

'But,' Simon demurred, 'there are so many things . . . .'

'The business of this great house runs smooth as a millrace and that is due to your diligence and foresight. One half a day. It is important work and there is no-one better skilled to do it.'

'Brother Orion, you were born with a silver tongue in your mouth.'

So, having prayed first, they went to Brother Kitchen who provided them with a viaticum of bread and a little cheese, and they set out. With the breeze now on their left they bent to the steep slope, not hurrying for it was a long climb. It warmed them.

'The new grinding-stone must be sent for as soon as possible. Some responsible person must go who understands what is needed, perhaps you, Brother Orion. But the Abbot will not give permission for this journey while winter still watches us. It is a long way.'

Half-way to the top, where the track turned off to the west, they stopped for a moment on a level. Over their heads the pilibeens flapped their weary wings and cried. The Abbey lay spread out below in the valley, between Duiske and Barrow, and the land rose gently from it on every side. All its buildings were clear to see in the thin air, the casa and infirmary near the river, the great cloister-garth – biggest in Ireland it was said – with the church closing it to the north. *Vallis Sancti Salvatoris.* Chaunticleer called from the barnyard, a tiny distant sound. They moved on; up here there was no hiding from that bitter wind that dried all before it, dried the sap in the branch, the marrow in the bone.

It was a good journey but it took a long time. Stumbling home much later through the chilly dark, Simon could not put his thumb on what it was that had caused it to take so long. He decided to put off thinking about it until a better time. He was cheered by the presence of Orion at his side, swinging along tirelessly and singing, what was it? 'Deirim dán ón deirim dán, an tráth a bhíonn mo bholg lán,' but Simon's knowledge of Irish did not permit him to translate. If it was a psalm it was one that Simon was not familiar with. What a cheerful heart, what a good companion!

They had not travelled far that morning when they came to a smoky clearing among the trees. Beside them was the charcoal-burners' hut, conical, made of tall poles and roofed with sods. In the middle of the clearing, one of the men stood high atop his mound while the smoke swirled around him before drifting away into the forest. He gestured to them with his long pole and when he smiled at them his eyes and teeth showed white in the dark face. Later they had come on two wood-cutters. Around them for a distance the wild birds had fallen silent, even the garrulous jays. The floor was white with fresh wood-chippings. Orion had asked to be allowed to use an axe. He laid aside his cloak and girded up his habit and attacked the tree with swinging strokes. Simon hadn't realized before what a powerful young man this was. The axe seemed but a goose-quill in his hands yet each curving blow sank into the wood to a hand's breadth and wedges of timber flew out. Orion breathed deeply but he was not distressed, and he never ceased until he motioned to them to stand out of harm's way, then a few more strokes and the top swayed across the clouds and the massive trunk came tearing and splintering to the forest floor. Simon was full of admiration; he loved the forest but he was no woodsman. Orion handed back the axe, wiped his forehead and resumed his cloak.

'Thank you.' He was smiling widely. 'Thank you.'

They had spent an hour, perhaps more, searching for tall masts among the trees on Brandon's western flank. Three they needed, and they must be tall, straight and strong. They found two and, having marked well the place, they padded down the slope, the soft leaf-carpet giving gently beneath their sandals. Pale bars of sunlight slanted in among the trunks. In a while there came in view a little house with a sagging thatch. As they approached it, a scurrying and scuffling seemed to take place as though someone, unseen, was upset at their coming; but very soon several men appeared and welcomed the two travellers who were brought in and put near the fire. Food was given them, cups of beer were passed round. The leader was a tall red-haired man who laughed a great deal so that his beard shook. Orion and the others talked like old acquaintances but as they spoke quickly in Irish, Simon understood no word of it, so he put off his cloak and leaned against the wall in the pleasant glow of the fire.

Looking back now, he thought that that was when their day had begun to slip from their grasp.

Through a hole in the thatch the sky looked in and after some time he noticed that the light was fading, so he tugged Orion's sleeve.

'It is time to go. We have many miles to travel.'

But Orion took Simon's empty cup and put instead a full one into his hand and taking him aside spoke very earnestly: 'We must not offend these good men.'

'But the Rule –,' he remonstrated.

'The Rule, Brother Simon, envisages perfection as indeed is right. It takes little account of reality. Our good Abbot in the casa may practise perfection; we must be in the world. Lambs must be born, fish must be gutted, calves castrated – the Abbot knows of such things but we are involved in them. We strive, we reach upward, reality jostles us. These poor people who scatter the brown grain or bend their backs to the sickle, the Abbot prays for their welfare, but he does not meet them and could not speak to them if he did. *We have seen their children sick, we have bound them up when they returned with savage wounds from cattle-raids, we have tied them with ropes and have sat on them to hold them down, hearing their screams while Brother Barber cut off the mangled limb.* Ah no! Perfection is for cold men in stone cells. We . . . ,' he shook his head. 'Drink, Brother Simon. These men are our friends.'

There was a piper, too, who played. With Orion's help he asked the piper, 'What is your song?'

'I sing of men and women, of my lord and his lady, of my lord's forefathers even to Adam, his battle-triumphs, his flocks and cattle and his wide lands. I sing too of the monks who tell the holy office. And of my friends who drink here with me and laugh. What else is there to sing?'

It was a merry gathering and but for the Rule he could have enjoyed it. 'What is time for but to waste' – was that Orion? who else would speak in Latin? – he leaned his head against the wall and sleep took gentle hold of him.

When he wakened a star was winking through the thatch,

the fire was out, the company gone. Orion stood in the doorway and pointed to the west, so Simon said, 'Lord, prosper them in their enterprise,' and then they set out, walking swiftly and hardly noticing the rough places although now it was quite dark. Sometimes Orion steadied Simon with a helping hand, and once he tripped on a fallen tree-branch, but he was not injured and they laughed as he picked himself up again. Orion told him the story of Ruadhán, who had an elm-tree from which flowed a fine beer. Of all the monks of Ireland, Ruadhán was the most loved. They found it a very good story.

After perhaps an hour's walking they reached the coomb where the sheep were gathered and would continue to be gathered each night until all the lambs were born and the danger of snow and blizzard had passed. The place had been chosen well. Steam rose from the hundreds of sheep that sheltered in an opening between two hills, their bawling filled the night, their woolly white gleamed dully, a hot smell was on the air. A fire glowed near the shepherd's hut that had been built under a bank, but the shepherd was away on his rounds. One of his dogs growled at them but when Orion spoke it wagged its tail and trotted beside them until they crossed the stream and went in among the trees again. It was level now. The track ran along the flank of Brandon through thin bare oaks, the hill lifting to their left, on their right falling away to the river. Around them the muted sounds of the night, their sandals noiseless on the mossy path. Far across the valley vixen barked, her voice carrying clear over the frosty distance; dog-fox answered. They felt the way at last dip down before them and knew they would soon be home. They were quiet, their talking all done, though sometimes Orion hummed a little cheerful tune. On the fringes of the thinning forest a white ghost startled them. Cat-head, a feathery bundle of silence, drifted by. So he would drift through the night until the moon-eyes caught a glint of movement, then the bundle became a pounce of tearing energy and a small life ended in a scream.

Their tired feet were glad of those last downhill miles until at last, Duiske crossed, they came to the final level and the stone arms reaching out in welcome.

It was not until the following day that it occurred to Simon to wonder why those men of Uí Dróna had been gathered there and why at fall of dark they had pushed even farther away from their own lands. He had bumped into a tall red-haired man who came round the corner of the infirmary. The stranger glanced at Simon, offered no apology, and as he turned away towards the eastern gate his beard shook with laughter. Brother Hippocrates, the sub-cellarer, did not know the stranger's name.

'A small matter . . . a broken finger. They say', he added in a whisper, 'that some of de Prendergast's beasts were driven last night. Ó Maolriain's men, so they say.'

Simon decided not to mention any of these things at Chapter. He sought out Brother Anselm who was learned in law and was glad when Anselm agreed. Anselm indeed was rather alarmed.

'You are in a sense an accessory or might be held to be so, and for that reason liable to arrest. Tell no-one.' Simon did not consider it necessary to pass on this advice to Orion.

That east wind could not blow for ever from Blackstair, snow-flecked. The rain came, grudgingly at first, then steadily. The wind now blew from Brandon and all the fountains were unlocked. The earth gulped down that cold wine, drank and drank until Duiske turned brown and their cloister-garth was a net of puddles. The change gave Simon the opportunity of attending to the stores, neglected whenever the weather allowed him to be out. In the gloomy cavernous store-rooms he noted the amount and condition of flour, of fish, of beer. Careful buying of salted pilchards during the season meant that the Brothers' diet was adequate if monotonous. Their bread ration had had to be reduced because of the great quantity of wheat the Abbot had shipped to England – no doubt it was being consumed at the campfires of the King's army in Scotland. Luce or salmon varied the meals. Of cheese they had a sufficiency. He tried to spend one day in the week at this work and kept his books scrupulously, otherwise three weeks' supply of food and drink had a way of being used in a fortnight. Bunches of seed-heads hung in cloth bags from nails in the beams; with Brother John's help he took these down, separated the seed from the withered stalks and having put each in its named box – onion, cabbage, lettuce, pease, beans – he brought the boxes to Agapanthus. Behind a loose stone in the wall he found a cache of beans and dried fish, stored no doubt against the pangs of Lent. He did not need to ask John or anyone else who had put them there; he sometimes felt that Brother Orion was not entirely fitted for the monastic discipline. After long hesitation he replaced the food in its hiding-place, and for a week afterwards gave back part of his bread in penance for his sin.

He had the fowl-houses cleaned and lime-washed; the fowl clucked disapprovingly and only with much murmuring did they consent to re-enter their unfamiliar home, but the rain decided them.

It was the month of Easter. There came a great upburst and greening so that when the rains ceased, of a sudden the miracle had happened once more and winter was finally routed. The sky was blue and mild, crows swaying in the trees, slender new growth everywhere, the last chevron of wild geese pointed north steering by glint of Barrow far below. The glorious sun looked into the huge bowl set in a meander of the Barrow, *Vallis Sancti Salvatoris*; it warmed and cheered all men and their labours prospered. Spring strode the furrows, soon all their sowing would be done. But Simon worried about that millstone. The Abbot had given no sign.

The Great Festival came. They put behind them fast and penance and for one day made a feast. The Brothers were to have a portion of fish or meat, double the daily beer-ration and the mugs with the handles, while there was also a rumour of a pudding though Brother Kitchen was not sure if the fruit could be sufficiently revived from its extreme desiccation. They sang their Lauds with fervour and when the last Amen had drifted up to heaven each in turn prostrated himself before the cross, the long aisle with its tamed but still-resonant stone now strangely silent.

Two days after Easter Simon was sent for and received his instructions from the Abbot. The following morning as the cock was crowing he and Orion set out on their mission. When the dawn came, cool and tender, they had already left the Abbey out of sight. Wild things ran away from striding feet, the sun lifted the dew from the grass up into the sparkling air. Like countrymen bred they walked with their eyes on the ground but missing nothing around, aware of the stirring, of the sap that drove up, up from the rotted darkness of the woodland into the limpid blue. Everything was young. The nestlings opened their yellow-rimmed mouths, bright eyes peered from every tree. A blackbird sang, each note rounded like a raindrop, spilling his shower of song on the air, drenching them with his music.

'There is still an hour to top of tide,' their boatman told them. He brought them into his home near the river where his wife gave them pitchers of buttermilk. A shower darkened the sun; when it ended they went through a glistening water-meadow and reached their boat. A moorhen skittered across the reedy backwater with a startled cry. They stowed their small wares and all was ready. Simon spoke the prayers, Orion dried the wet planks with his sleeve before sitting in the stern, Fergus pushed off.

Their voyage took them through the wide valley of the Barrow, the tide their ally, ducks going up in a clatter of wings from the reed-beds, an otter slipping away from them with only a whisker showing above his curling wave. Brandon kept them company, then flattened and vanished.

A grey heron fished the shallows. Coots spread their white tails and sailed before the wind. Ripple and drift, rowing was an easy task, and they took turns at the oars, pausing only at the prescribed times to pray. A breeze cooled them and ruffled the water. Saint Moling's broken tower and its green hummock were a familiar landmark but soon they reached areas known only to their boatman. He told stories about places they passed, why the names, hero-stories, who had hunted here, who had loved, had fought, had died, and some of the stories Orion translated. He spoke of the twelve battles that the Leinstermen had broken on Uí Néill. 'And it was Éanna Cinnsealach who won them all.' Simon saw the brightness fall in drops from the blade, dip, grip, heave, and the river push the oar again away and up into the clean air to drip, drip, while their boat cut a sibilant path into the south. He listened to the oarsman's voice, knowing a word here and there, and wished he had mastered this language, so light and swift.

The Nore met them and journeyed on with them. It was a prim river, coming from its wooded slopes, its cloisters and townships, and it sang a different song, but it was welcomed by the generous Barrow. Then came Rosponte, with its great bridge and bustling wharves heaped with corded bales.

High on a windy ridge above the river they found the stone-men. Simon went with them to choose their block of stone, then the master pegged his centre, stretched his line and, following Brother Simon's directions and dimensions, scribed his circle. His commission fulfilled, Simon left them to their patient pecking and took himself away across the hill; below he could see the wide waters where the Three Sisters met and showed their pleasure by leaping at one another and tossing their white hair, while on the farther bank, quite clear, was the abbey of *Sancta Maria* at Dunbrody, on the green level just above the flotsam of flood-tide. How far was it? A mile or two? Because the land fell away so steeply and because of that broad expanse of restless water, it was difficult to tell. But it was a world away; he had never been there.

'Fergus tells me he has fishing rights on the east bank opposite his home. Before our Abbey's foundation these rights were given to a kinsman of Fergus's by Mac Murrough. The Abbey cannot challenge that.'

Simon looked questioningly into Orion's clear blue eyes.

'The Abbey', Orion amended, 'would find it difficult to oppose; the difficulty would be out of proportion to the possible advantage gained.'

Simon nodded doubtfully.

Fergus was waiting patiently at the quay. They negotiated shallows and backwaters until the incoming sea caught them and their cot was swept upriver between the muddy shelves of the indolent Suir. The city squatted dark on the darkening river-bank, grim-walled and towered. Masts stood against the western light. A cold breeze declared that spring could still be held at bay or even turned back.

Fergus pointed towards the setting sun.

'Many a mile west along the river is Inishlounachta, the old abbey of the Suir. I have been there. It sits on the flat land by the river-edge, in the golden land of Munster, a place of milk and honey.'

Neither of the Brothers had seen it.

Having spent the night at the Nunnery on the northern shore and successfully completed their business on the following day, they were carried by the ebbing tide down the broad Suir back again to the junction of the three great rivers where Waterford haven opened to the south, and there they rested and ate. When it came it was a strong tide and Fergus did what rowing was needed. Simon, dozing on the stern-seat, felt about his waist the unaccustomed weight of the fat money-belt. Memories of their meeting with the Italians came to him; the wind had risen strongly in the night so that the ships pitched and tossed their masts at the clouds and the ragged crows were flung across the sky; the rope ladder at the ship's side, so difficult for landsmen, the courteous welcome, the creaking cabin with its sloping timbers burnished; Signor Lucca sitting at the chart-table, leaning back in his chair and allowing Signor Perone to lead the negotiations but now and then putting in a word or asking for a document. Signor Polo they hardly saw; he scratched on parchment with a long feather and kept his bald head down. Simon had had an uneasy sleep in a soft bed; lack of sleep sometimes leaves the mind emptied and concentrated, and so he had found it on this occasion and was glad of it. He had also had the aid of the Prior's meticulous figures.

All had gone well. They had settled and signed. They had drunk a glass of wine and had shaken hands very cordially. One of the sailors who stood guard outside the door was sent to fetch the Captain, whom they thanked; then there were gifts for the Captain, for Signor Lucca, for the elder Lucca who no longer ventured abroad, for the Abbot and the Prior. Simon with firm courtesy refused the jar of wine with which the merchants wished to present him.

When they left the sunless cabin and stooped out the narrow door it had seemed odd to find the bright day waiting for them and the high clouds racing before the wind.

He was asleep and had to be roused at their place of disembarking. Handing up Orion's pack he asked, 'What makes your pack so heavy, Brother?' but Orion appeared not to hear the question. They warmly thanked their boatman, not even once looking in the direction of his fish-traps, then set off to tramp the mile or so to the Abbey. The uncurling bracken crunched under their feet and the clover globes coloured the meadows. It transpired that Orion *had* heard: 'It is a jar of Tuscan wine. The Italian was most pressing.'

Simon was glad to lean on his staff, but the young man used his to swipe at dandelions and send the golden discs whirling. How marvellous is youth and strength!

He went at once to the casa to hand over the money and documents, and was relieved that their commission had been successfully completed. Then they joined their Brethren at Compline.

When at last the millstone arrived, a work-party had been mustered at the point on the Barrow where the tide's attack finally spent itself and broke on the rapids of Carriglade. The barge was poled into position under the sheerlegs; with infinite care the stone was lifted and swung round. When it rested firmly on the ground it was brought to the vertical and a stout pole pushed through. Now began the slow rolling of the wheel along the river path, three men under each end of the pole. As they approached the narrowest place, where the hill pushed out towards the river, they stopped to rest and while two of the men changed positions Simon passed them on the river side in order to get before them on the road. His back was turned so that he did not see what happened – a stumble or perhaps a sudden cramp, or maybe it was the fault of the squirrel that dropped from a branch and ran across their path – he heard the confused noise, the yell of warning, looked up to see the leviathan thundering down on him, said an un-Cistercian word, and jumped. His foot caught in a log on the brink and he splashed into the shallows. The great wheel hit the log, bounded high, and whirled out into the deeper water, and a wave sprang six cubits into the air to make room for it.

III
EARTH

W HAT is time for but to use, he reminded himself, and hurried, though it was too warm to hurry. He brushed through forests of wild parsley and stitchwort, and the whole world was white with May. On the sloping flank of Coppanagh a sparrowhawk quartering the hillside swung low over the furze. The chestnut candles were all alight. Big stout lambs in the fields, still with their dams, he paused to count, and a lark sang invisible.

In the glade called Tubbrid he threw himself down beside the well where the grass was cool, balanced himself, leaned down and gulped mouthfuls of that intoxicating coldness, straightened up then to get his breath, enjoying the dribbling down his beard down his neck down his chest. The bubbles scurried to the surface of the water and burst into the air; he watched narrowly but could not see where they started among the stones and grey sand. Ferns leaned out from the edge to dip their fronds in life and near where he kneeled a tiny wave bulged and came tumbling through a runnel in the stone. The smell of the broken garlic leaves was about. He wet his finger among fallen petals, made the sign of the cross and thanked the creator of water and of wells.

How different his return. Worried, chastened, he sought out first the Prior and told his tidings. The Prior's usually pale face became pink and damp; he twisted his fingers together in agitation.

'Brother Michael thinks it was MacGiolla Pádraig's men. But Brother Grangemaster says that sheep are beneath MacGiolla Pádraig's attention. Indeed most of the damage is to fences and crops. The plough-oxen are safe.'

'What is the value of the three sheep?'

'Perhaps two shillings.' The Prior took his quill and wrote; it was his answer to most problems.

'There is also the corn, beer and oil.'

'In all?'

'Let us say five shillings.'

'It is a sad loss. We ought to tell the Abbot?' he said doubtfully.

'May I suggest how we might proceed?' Simon asked.

'Of course, of course.' He seemed much relieved.

'The Earl should be informed. His men of Gowran must see to it. That, however, would be for the Abbot, who is most intimate with the Earl. There is also another course of action which might be taken. It is in Ó Maolriain's interest that raids by outlaws be guarded against, since he too has many cattle. And Vallis Dei is close to the territory he regards as his.'

'Where is this territory?'

'North of Sruhaunglórach, to the east of the Barrow. But he also claims lands north of Vallis Dei. As you know, our grange of Vallis Dei was founded on lands granted by an ancestor of Ó Maolriain.'

'How do these arrogant claims lie beside the rights of the Earl?'

'The two might be likened to the cat and the dog who doze, old enemies, on opposite sides of the hearth, each with an ear cocked. The prudent householder needs both of them to guard his house.'

'How do we speak with Ó Maolriain?'

'Through our Brother Orion, whose relationship with Ó Maolriain, though in a sense sinister, can be at times most valuable.'

Thus it was agreed.

He hurried then to the cloister, its arches gilded by the summer sun. Father Gout sat in a niche near the chapter house, old bones taking comfort from the warmth. He

listened calmly as though the story too was old.
'On your way to the grange of *Vallis Dei*?'
'Yes. At the eel-weir. The northern weir.'
'I know it well.'
'The yellow flags were in bloom in the damp places. Water-hens clucked and scuttled in the reeds.'
'I remember.'
'Her little feet left no prints in the water. Only wet prints in the grass.'
'You did well to come to me. We depend on you. You are the Lord Abbot's right hand.'
'She came towards me out of the river.'
'You knew her?'
'The tanner's daughter.'
'Did you not turn away?'
'There was not time. I hid that she might not blush. She waded towards me; her thighs were sleek and wet; she spread her white arms wide for balance as she stepped flinching on the pebbles.'
'Ah!'
'Her hair hung damp about her white shoulders. She reached a grassy place, stood there then with the sun on her, and a blackbird sang, opening coloured lips.'
'And then?'
'I could not look. I looked down. Her toes and little round heels made wet stars among the grasses and the water dripped from her.'
Father Gout looked across the sun-warmed garth at the plots of fennel and rue, rosemary, thyme and sweet marjoram that throve happily there, at the edges and arcs of amber stone that had sailed across the sea from Simon's own land, that had floated up the river, that newly shaped and turned had been flung up into the air to sing God's praise, and that rested now in the sun unaware both of their burden and of their own massive strength, clean and sharp still as when the mason had laid down his chisel; at the shadowed

colonnades where for sixty years he himself had made one shadow more. He began as he always began: 'There is no abiding evil in doing wrong, for man is weak. The evil lies in not repenting'; this gave him time for thinking. He looked up at Simon and smiled. 'Give me your arm, Brother.'

Once on his feet he could keep moving without much difficulty, Simon supporting him.

They paused a moment where Brother Scribe had set his easel. Beside him stood two younger men who held inks, colours, knives and many feathered brushes. Brother Scribe feared that soon his eyes would no longer hold their sharp edge and he was most anxious that all he knew of his craft be passed on, but certainly there was as yet no lessening of his mastery, as Simon could clearly appreciate from his glance at the parchment. The hand and the eye that work together in cunning, knowing right, knowing beauty – this Simon greatly admired, this skill, all dextrous gifts, he revered.

'Yet grant me, Lord, to love also those who have *no* skill, the plough-oxen of the world. Give me,' he prayed humbly, 'give me at last the high grace of indifference so that black and white may be alike grey to me.'

When they continued their ambulation, the old man said, 'Since to fly the temptation might have caused more scandal than to stay hidden, you need not confess publicly in Chapter – indeed that in itself might cause scandal. Let us return.' So they turned again along the northern side, silent as they passed a group of Brethren who were gathering around a lectern where Brother Anselm waited. 'The situation was not of your seeking. However, to discipline the flesh you will fast on bread and water for ten days and you will perform all your duties with even more diligence than usual, in order not to allow time for idle thoughts.'

Simon's suggestion of a diplomatic approach to their northern neighbour was approved. He and Orion left at first light. The cocks sang their rousing song. The lark leapt into the sky. The culver-house opened its arms and flung out a swarm of wings. By the great oak-wood with its lake of bluebells, by Ullard's ancient church, following the river north, was a walk of about six miles. Bees sucked in the clover flowers. A hawk hung in the air watching all of Uí Dróna. Orion thought there never could be time enough for hay-fields, for summer a-loll and a-sprawl, for pools of amber water and spidered wells, all the summers he had known rolled together into a dozen images of joy. Swan, flower-white, drifted, one above, one below, drifted, one in the leaf-green air, one in ale-brown water, arched regal neck and reached down to the mirror, the other reached up, they kissed. He stood motionless on a flat rock at morning, a willow rod in his hand, and watched the shadowed water. When a trout came up he smacked the water sharply with the rod and the poor trout, shocked, turned up its white belly, while he leaned down and flicked it out onto the bank. A black shining beetle lit and burned in the sunlight. The air was drowsy with the heavy, warm smell of the yellow furze, that smell of summer noons. Ahead, a small herd of deer moved like pale wraiths among the young trees of Silaire, keeping their distance, aware but unafraid, until Orion ran at them with a yell and a bellow of laughter, and they floated away seeming hardly to touch the bluebells that covered the floor of the forest.

At the village Brother Orion had calls to make which, he suggested gently, he could do best on his own. So Simon walked by the stream and kneeled beside a grey boulder to pray. On the far bank a red fox came down to drink; he lapped daintily, his pink tongue and sharp white fangs showing; some hint of danger sent him slipping away, turning to grin into Simon's eyes before disappearing among the towering spears of the lady fingers.

Orion's messenger was a dark-eyed child who came very shyly to tug at Simon's sleeve. Simon put his finger to his lips then pointed downstream. The water curled languidly round the stems where the jewelled dragon-flies hovered;

beyond the yellow flags, halcyon perched on a twig, humped his blue shoulders and peered into the stream, spear-beak at the ready. Watch well now, little hunch-back! Mid-summer, blue on blue, the living is easy, yet this meal depends on your concentration. All of you, just a handful of feathers and colour sharpened to an eye and a beak, crouched there above the smooth gliding water that you pierce with your gaze, king of fishers.

He followed the boy back to the village and though he used his full stock of Irish he got no response but an uncertain smile. Here the Brethren were given bread hot off the griddle on which the butter melted and ran, and methers of beer; Simon knew now that he must not refuse, and noticed Orion looking at him approvingly. The owner of the cottage was a man who worked at harvest-time at the Old Grange, the two other men were strangers. The woman who had made the bread smiled and smiled but did not speak, and after some time the dark-eyed boy and his baby sister came and put their hands into Simon's hand, which pleased him enormously.

When they left, the beetle was droning in the dusk. They reached home with the first star.

IV
HARVEST

PROMISE of plenty rippled across the fields of grain. Blue-necked swayed the wheat, carrying the world on its slender shoulders. There were thickets of woodbine and dogrose, meadow-sweet in waves of perfume, the smell of honey, the smell of sun-ripened bracken. Scarlet poppies blazed and pale convolvulus clambered among the leaning stalks. Orion exulted. It was for this he lived: to loll and laze in sunny meads, make time stand still while corncrake and wood-quest sang sleepily and fairy thimbles drove up purple through the grasses. The pulse of summer made a song sweeter than fingers on strings of music. Warm days, nights of dew, and already the barley was bronzing.

A message came by devious ways to Simon. Whence it came, by whom brought, were unclear but its import was sufficiently clear. It caused him to smile wryly. 'No disturbance of the peace of the Abbey's granges by robbers or other evilly disposed persons would be tolerated. Perhaps the Abbey would be willing to make certain provision for the sustenance of those whose vigilance would keep the granges inviolate. The terms of this latter arrangement would no doubt be amenable to amicable agreement.' He knew this would entail long and delicate negotiations, and his time was occupied now with a great project, that of raising the millstone. It had come to rest on a sandy bar; their thorough examination showed it to be undamaged; every day of sun and night of dreaming stars brought it closer to the surface of the river till one rim of it showed.

Once again the heavy masts were moved and set asplay above the stone, their feet firm in gravel and mud. The river resisted, tugged and sucked to hold on, but was at last forced to yield up its prize which hung there dripping while the two boats moved in underneath to take its weight. They hauled the load to where Duiske spilled into Barrow, brought the wheel ashore and this time accomplished without mishap the final stages of the task.

It was time to test the working of the mill, to tighten or loosen as might be needed. Soon there would be no time; the cares of the harvest would keep every able-bodied person busy from dawn to sunset. Simon sought out Brother Timothy and they set out along the *Via Magna*. Still, with a filmy sunshine, the air alive with the hum of many insects. A wheel of thistledown drifted past. The big butterflies with the purple spots were flopping around in the sun. Lazy things, just sitting in the sun, on the knapweed, slowly opening and closing their wings. To reach the mill-bridge the two monks pushed through a forest of bracken, head-high. When they had painstakingly tested and proved all, Simon sighed with satisfaction. Again they kneeled on the floor and gave their thanks and both thought of the other time so many months before, when they had kneeled so. 'All things come with patience. Grant me, Lord, that happy gift.' He smiled at Timothy, then looked out the narrow window where in the east Blackstair tilted towards the sun. It was August and the loosestrife was purpling the bogland; summer was on the turn. Earth laughed and corn fattened.

Autumn came, dappled, appled. Brown fat spiders swung on gossamer, speckled spinners of gnat-nets. Berries gleamed black-purple, burned amid the spears of the holly. Orion loved the harvest-time; he turned his face to the damp dawn holding his sickle in his right hand, his wooden rake across his shoulder. He must be first in the field, even before the dews had dispersed, to see to it that every arm was marshalled for the onslaught. He had left Brother Simon to consign workers to the various tasks, to make sure of horses, oxen, wagons, to see that bread and beer found its way to every work-party, to check barrels, store-rooms and barns. The Prior no doubt was at his desk, sharpening quills, but Orion would bend his back and swing his sickle, lead all by example, would sweat and burn, bend and swing till shoulder and arm and back ached, and then would tramp home at dusk, hugely content, to sleep, sleep, sleep, without glimmer of dream, without stir, like a sheaf in the stubble. Sometimes he left his sickle and took a turn at binding the sheaves, or threw them up into stooks so that sun and wind could sift through and leave them dry for stacking. *Nemo dat quod non habet.* He helped wherever help was needed, admonished, encouraged, told them stories, laughed with them, and when at last he straightened to look around at the dark stacks leaning their shadows away from the silent-rising moon, feeling the blessing of the dew on his hot forehead, knowing that one more field was safe, he felt a huge unhumble strength flow through his chest and shoulders and thighs, and knew he could accomplish anything.

'We start an hour later tomorrow,' he told them, but in the night it rained so everyone had respite. Standing in the doorway of the barn he watched the raindrops glisten and swell and drip along the lintel and was doubly glad that they had stayed late the previous night to finish. His fingers tingled and smarted from the thistle thorns, but that was a small thing when all that corn was snug and dry.

There was no further interruption to their work, except for a black storm of thunder and warm heavy rain that drenched one Sunday after Nones and then raced away to sulk and grumble in the hills, leaving the earth and the roofs steaming; by the sixth hour on the following day it was dry enough to begin again, and Brother John that same week began drawing in. The field opened its generous arms, gave up its gift then lay back exhausted, quiet and emptied, rifled of its gold, left to fieldmouse and woodquest and quail, while the army of harvesters moved on. He thought of the creaking wagons, of the girls who came gleaning, of trudging through day's end to the street of flagons, to find his way at last by the stone stairway and fall exhausted onto his bed. It was the weather that decided when they started or stopped; there were mornings of drenching dew when they could not begin; they sometimes worked till the stars stood on the sky; often he was old with weariness but always exultant. Youth and health and strength are pride.

He walked beside the last slow wagon, one hand on the rope that held the rustling fragrant load. The oxen complained windily and Brother Edwin touched them with his long willow rod but did not hurry them because now there was no need. Smoke curled up from the cottages outside the gate; children played; a woman washed clothes in Duiske stream; a boy and girl were whispering where the hazels hung; the world was about its business.

There was now a different task, one for which they had long been preparing. *Vallis Sancti Salvatoris* had indeed in a sense been a hundred years preparing for this day. All the Lord Abbot's invitations had long since been delivered and answered, the church fresh whitewashed and all the monastic buildings repaired and cleaned.

Simon went with the Prior through the gardens and by way of the slype into the arcaded peace of the cloister. Though it was a day of bustling winds, in here it was still; around this hub of quiet the busy life of the Abbey turned. A Brother was working in the church; he polished the wooden stalls until they shone like chestnuts fresh out of their shells, and as each one was finished he stood back to admire it then kneeled to offer a prayer, his polishing rag in one hand, his jar of beeswax in the other. Simon could not see his face. The Prior unlocked the door at the bottom of the caracole, locked it behind them, then as they climbed the stair chose from the jangling ring another key for the door of the tower, and they stepped in. Here were kept their legal documents, the closely written pages of the *Articuli*, grants of lands, the deeds that conferred its privileges on the Abbey, the sacred vessels not in use and the *Sigillum* and Charter for which they had come. The windows had been boarded and the light was dim. The wind moaned softly through the chinks. In the room above them was the uneasy fluttering of many wings. The doors were locked again behind as they descended, bringing with them the Great Seal and Charter which they lodged in the chapter house.

Victuals were all in readiness, venison, honey, beer, mead and metheglin, fowls roast and boiled, woodcock and quail, milk, butter, curds and cheese, wild pig and beef. Bread would be baked during the night that it might be brought hot to table. There were pewter and brass, goblets of wood or horn, and on the high table tall glasses for the wines brought from France and Italy. Their best lambs had been slaughtered, there were eels and salmon from the Barrow. The fasting would come afterwards, but for this one day they would feast and remember the twelve who had come down the shoulder of Coppanagh and had set the first corner-stone by Duiske in a loop of the Barrow.

Such to-ings and fro-ings, such arrivals and dismountings, such scanning of horizons, such last-minute tasks to send them scurrying. A breeze sprang up and bundled the clouds away. It sent the song of the bell all through the valley. Through the glistening grass the hooves came in to Duiske from north, south, east and west.

As the hour approached, the Abbot with Bishop Chever beside and his Seniores grouped around him, the Prior and all the choir-monks too, waited in welcome. Word came flying: the Earl's party had been seen, first their colours, then their hoof-beats and then they were advancing at a stately pace down the final slope. The Earl sat straight and dignified. Cuirass and poitrel gleamed, the gilt and crimson aprons jerked in time with the palfreys' hooves, above and about them a thicket of spears, while pennons whipped in the brisk air that blew from the river.

Ó Maolriain's arrival was different. It was casual and almost unnoticed, a flurry near the northern gate, the hunting-dogs trotting at the horses' heels. He rode without saddle or bridle, arrogant, sitting slightly sideways, consciousness of power in the lift of his jaw, the glance that rested carelessly on the throng. Those nearer him saw, and some with surprise, that he was of only average height, lean, with a face too narrow to be handsome, and hard grey eyes. Here, he was within the orbit of power of the Earl, but he showed no hint of unease; those about him were picked men who saw everything for him.

Brother Simon having seen the Earl's party to their places returned to find his services were needed again. He stepped forward with words of welcome, embraced Ó Maolriain and together they entered the cool dim church.

The Earl knelt at his prie-dieu. The other guests were also in their allotted places. The vacant prie-dieu was perhaps a sword's length farther from the altar. Ó Maolriain stiffened and stopped like a hunting-dog that scents a quarry.

'Our Abbey's land is from the Earl,' Simon hastened to explain. 'As is our charter.'

He spoke quietly but Ó Maolriain's answer was louder: 'A scrap of vellum that is not proof against a candle-flame. As to the land, before this Earl was known, when his fathers ran barefoot, the land was ours. Before Christ died, it was Uí Dróna.'

Simon threw a scared glance at the Earl – the Earl's head was bowed in his hands – then an equally startled glance at MacGiolla Pádraig, at de Prendergast, at the tall figure of old Sir Thomas de Cantwell. Ó Maolriain noticed, and the ghost of a sour smile crossed his thin face - this poor foreigner, what did he know?

Simon looked round in dismay. He was on his own. Abbot and Prior were robing. Then the cheerful face of Orion, a whisper in Simon's ear. Orion bowed to Ó Maolriain then raised his head and smiled straight into the angry face. Ó Maolriain had seen those blue eyes before. Orion spoke softly, gesturing towards the high altar, then took the other gently by the arm and led him unresisting to his prie-dieu.

What Simon remembered afterwards most clearly was the immense throng that gave a grave motion to the church, a solemn whisper that underlay the voices of the monks. The windows above the altar showed ribbons of sky, but inside was the smudged gleam of candles, the purples and the cloth of gold, the lawns and damasks, the silver backed by the dark stone on which white tapers shone, the incense, the music, the familiar Latin made strange by these strange circumstances, the bells, the assault of prayer that lifted as though there were no roof up into the heavens to batter at the gates. But the crowd, with its sway and murmur, like a tide at the full, *that* he remembered most.

Then came Michaelmas. Again the crowds, even greater crowds. While it was still night they were on the road, by foot, by hoof, by wheel, from the fat lands of the valley, from rock and heather, from both sides of Barrow and from the marches. From the four shires they hurried, stepping briskly across the stubble-lands or by the margins of the forests; no doubt from places farther off, from the cities too and from humbler places, Kilcolumb, Ullard, Gowran.

There was rain early and all the ways were damp but soon the sun slipped over the hills. The busy breeze herded the showers away.

Roped across the bosom of the river a necklet of boats swayed and tugged, a vast bawling of beasts was hunted into the water, poked and prodded, led across by a rope tied from a cot to the leader's horns. The trampled grass that six months later in memory could still be smelled, damp leather and clothes and hair, the smell of people, many people. Simon crossed by boat and walked quickly through the crowds. He caught sight of the minstrel who had the night before stayed in the hospice and who after Compline had carolled and played on the lute. *Heu alas pour amour*, he had songs in different tongues . . . *E les prestres, quan ont chante* . . . He had travelled in many lands, had been more than once to Paris, and only five years before as a boy had gone on the great pilgrimage to Rome to pay homage at the shrine of Saint Peter. Today he played at the fair; people stopped a while to listen but no crowd followed. Around the old harper, however, was an island of quiet and attention. He made the strings talk to them, sometimes adding his own words, the airs martial, or slow, or quick and dancing. Simon was impressed by the harper's skill and by his dignity. His squire was a roguish young fellow who laughed with the young people, and when the harper was resting the jolly squire played on his goatskin tambourin and his eyes sparkled at the sparkling eyes of the girls.

A man down from the hills had a wonder, a pony that danced. What a marvel! A white star blazed and when the pony sprang up on its dainty black hooves you saw its drawn-in belly, and all the thews and sinews of its legs where each one was set in, and all the curving muscles knotted together to form the slender fetlock and the huge haunches, rods of velvet that moved on one another. It showed its white eyes and flung up its mane and blew out its flaring nostrils. What beauty! Suddenly he was thinking again of the tanner's daughter. He rushed away from his thought, past bone-players and basket-makers, thimblers, tanglers and pedlars, and he found Brother Bursar still and watchful with his tally-boy where the fair revolved round them with shouting and music. Simon stood beside his Brother, just as gravely, so that all could see him: the symbol of the Abbey's privileges, of Lastage, Pontage, Stallage, Infangthef, Outfangthef, Wayf and Stray, Cornage, Elsilver and Brasinage, the Custody and Assay of Weights and Measures, a long list, many others too, all set down in documents – Toll, Passage, Pontage, Geldage, such a litany. He stood strong and solid as befitted one who represented religion and law, even when a dog snarled near him, when a rival rushed at the one that had snarled, and the two went twisting in a confusion of legs, tails and fierce white fangs, then as quickly separated and rushed away in mutual terror to opposite corners of the fair. He bowed in grave greeting to a young woman in scarlet shawl who sold lean athletic black hens. The hurdy-gurdy whirled its limping tunes. There was a stall where gaudies were for sale. Over the heads of the crowd he saw on a sloping park a game of hurling, young men in packs pursuing an unseen ball of wood or leather, roaring and hacking at shins with their crooked staves. A pedlar shouted his wares, simples for the relief of aching of the joints, for low fevers, for the ague, for the staggers, for the gout, an herb which was certain to cure sprains, bruises, lacerations, rheumatics or tightness of any kind, another (or was it the same?) which was warranted a sovereign specific for the looseness.

He saluted those passers-by whom he knew, 'Benedicite'. The tanner and his wife. Behind them their daughter, little hands folded before her, demure, nun-like, a lodestone for many eyes, her gaze cast down, a posy of flowers in the crook of her arm. Was her marriage settlement being arranged today? A puppy, lost, scampered out from among the feet, tumbled, squealed, rolled onto Simon's sandals and, liking that safe haven, made its water all over Simon's toes, and even then Brother Cellarer did not once look down. However, when the day became too warm they moved to the shade and sat on a log where they were joined by the Prior. Orion came and carried Simon away to greet the harper and the minstrel, who by now had met but were having problems in their different tongues. The two Brethren were drawn in to become part of the laborious chain of translation, but after struggling a while they found it too difficult and withdrew.

'There are, in any case, some matters to attend to,' Orion explained. 'There is a stranger who refuses stallage, you will know him, he sells fish. Near the great chestnut tree. Hold him in talk,' and he was gone.

Simon found the stranger, one who sold fish and oil, his counter the top of a salt-barrel, and spoke pleasantly to him, 'We have not before been honoured by your business.'

They discussed the pilchard-fishing, the difficulties of transport, and while the merchant talked, two familiar figures appeared and stood casually one on each side of him, while Orion stood behind. The merchant glanced uneasily at them.

'For you our toll is one half-penny.'

'Not . . . ,' said the merchant, and stopped.

The tall man who stood on his right laughed mirthlessly and his red beard shook; he allowed his cloak to fall aside to reveal a straight-bladed dagger in his belt. The fish-merchant looked to his left and found cold grey eyes watching him. There was no further trouble.

'There is also Aodh. He has his usual quibble. A man of law told him – so he says – that as he has no stall . . . And Mistress Pogue, the hen-wife. Perhaps you, Brother Cellarer, as a man of acute mind and skilled in diplomacy, might attend to Aodh?'

Aodh to be sure never missed a gathering such as this. His avocation was Prick-the-garter, and fair-day was his harvest.

'He should not prove difficult; he will wish to return.'

They saw that the crowd that had surrounded the harper was gone, and the two musicians had discovered that they understood one another without words, for music needs none. The harper listened, the troubadour sang, windows opened.

Orion helped Mistress Pogue to load her wares and went with her to her abode where she pleasured him in the hay and this he deemed a sufficient acknowledgment of the Abbey's prerogatives. The pecuniary loss to the Abbey's coffers was small, the accrual of good-will incalculable.

It was late before the fairground emptied. The Abbey was long sunk in sleep. The moon rose to shepherd home the last revellers.

V
HOME

SIMON set out on his visitation with a happy heart. The harvest had been bountiful, *Deo gratias*; Duiske once more ground his stone teeth, the meal poured out to fill sacks, barrels and panniers; all was well. Calm dry days blessed their journeying to the western granges and with Brother Timothy to help, assessment and auditing was quickly accomplished. The Killenny grange he left until last and brought Orion with him. Orion had many friends and relatives in that northern area and the Abbey wished to remain on the best of terms with Ó Maolriain on whose ancestral territory Killenny lay. And so they set out, through Silaire wood and by Ullard. The crisp leaves rustled, roving bands of finches flickered among the haws. A stag bellowed from the wooded rock above Clashganny. Orion would have dawdled, picked the last of the blackberries and sloes and hazels, but Simon would not have it. What is time for but to use? at which the young man looked at him and laughed.

When they reached *Vallis Dei*, however, there were disturbing tidings: two Brothers from Jerpoint had been there making inquiries and requesting hospitality, the old trouble showing again in a new and ambiguous way. He decided to make a very thorough inquisition; he saw all buildings, animals and foodstocks. He closely questioned the grange-master, and determined that when the Brothers then at the grange went back to the Abbey they should be replaced by three or perhaps four others, though there was little for them to do except to tend the sheep and cattle, mill whatever was needed and continue ploughing as the weather allowed. Two ricks of corn in outlying fields were to be at once drawn in and threshed, and when a supply of safe dry barrels had been sent from Duiske, the grain was to be returned in them, keeping at *Vallis Dei* only enough for their needs.

The weather changed. Their work was delayed by sweeping storms of rain. When it eased, Simon and Orion spent most of a day inspecting the flocks which were still scattered about the higher land. The raindrops hung from the thinning haws and shone on the hazel boughs with their few yellowed leaves and fresh green catkins. Everywhere damp; showers fell on their shoulders from the branches.

Then to the account-rolls, while outside the trees dripped and the puddles spread and the hills vanished behind curtains of grey. The third morning, however, dawned sharp and sunlit. Their work approached completion, but Simon was worried. The wind was keen and cold from the north through that unglazed window and there was ice in it. They finished; they debated; they had already spent so much more time here than intended, yet to start now at the ninth hour was to be soon overtaken by dark.

'If we go straight over the hill it will be a quick journey and we shall sing Vespers at *Sancti Salvatoris*,' and Simon allowed himself to be persuaded. Orion had the eagerness of a boy, and besides there was the strong pull of home.

The wind snapped at their heels as they crossed the level fields. The wet ground sucked down their feet and slowed them.

'We cannot follow the road in any case; the river fields are flooded,' so they started on the long slope, and now they found how cold it was and were glad they had their heavy woollen cloaks. Simon was glad too of his staff, but Orion used his to slice off briar-tips or to hurl bundles of wet leaves into the air, until the hill became too steep and then they both leaned into it. And while they struggled upwards with furze grabbing at their robes, Simon became uneasily aware of a change around them. He stopped, looked back.

'The wind?'

Orion nodded. The wind which had been at their backs when they left had slowly shifted north-west, but in the last few minutes out on the bare cheek of the mountain it had whipped around until it was on their left shoulder and the sky was beginning to darken sullenly.

'No time to lose.'

Stones slipped from under their feet where a steep path had been cut into channels by the rain. They found themselves in a thicket of stiff blackthorn that tore at their clothes and stabbed at faces and hands. Simon's ankle hurt where he had struck it against a rock. They pushed on, sure they would soon reach an end, but instead the thorns grew closer. At last, hot and sweating from stooping, parrying, dodging, yet making little progress, Orion stopped dead.

'This is foolish,' he said, panting, wiping sweat out of his eyes. 'We are not thinking.'

He looked at Simon, but Simon left decision to him. Orion peered around; eye ear nose, all senses sharpened to an edge, he crouched till he could see along the ground beneath the thorn bushes. Now that the pumping of his heart had calmed he could hear the wind moving above their heads, but he listened for another sound. Since the ground sloped slightly left they moved slowly in that direction, stopped, listened again, moved on and stumbled into a little gully with a trickle of water at the bottom of it. Orion grunted. They followed the water downhill to where it joined a stream, and the sound he had been seeking was clear enough now. The blackthorn did not grow beside the stream nor could it reach across from the high banks. They jumped from rock to tumbled rock down to the lower levels, and when at last they came out of the shelter of the ravine it was to find the bitter wind blowing straight into their faces.

'Dear God, help me to have patience with those whose vanity outweighs their knowledge. And to pay no attention to their advice,' Simon prayed silently.

He realized that what he had taken for the craft of the master pathfinder was not much more than pride in strength, the optimism and confidence of youth. No one must be asked to answer for more than one; he took command.

He looked around. The naked trees cowered and shivered; the grey ceiling had dropped lower and the night was almost come, an hour before its time.

'Let us find some place to rest. I am sure there are houses near.'

They were indeed close to the road that they would have travelled had they not decided to cross the mountain. Soon they came to a small hut huddled in a sheltered place, the wind whipping smoke from its squat chimney. The fire burned bright; they were welcomed and given a supper of oaten porridge. The man did all the talking for his wife and children, who sat in the yellow circle and watched the visitors shyly. When the fire died and only the back-log glowed in the dark room they stretched out to sleep on straw. Simon's ankle throbbed; he discovered it was swollen and tied it up tightly.

And while they slept the snow came white and stealthy. At dawn they looked out on a dazzling new world and Blackstair glinted under a red eastern sky. A huge silence had descended as though all the myriad mouths of the wilderness had been stopped.

There were four miles to travel. They were bad miles. The ways were foul. An icy wind tore at them. Simon's ankle became more painful the farther they went and he was glad of Orion's help at the more difficult places. All the river-plain lay under wrinkled sheets of water so that their own Barrow was a stranger. They had to keep to the higher levels and even here every step was ambushed by drift and rock and swollen streams.

Near Akylethawn they stopped while Simon re-tied the sopping cloth on his foot. They waited a moment in the lee of a ruined wall, tempted by the shelter, poor though it was, while the wolf-wind with fangs of ice moaned above them.

'Listen!'

They listened. Again across the snow-daubed valley sailed that thin cry, full of cold and hunger and primeval lifelust. Simon felt the hairs on his neck lift and looked in alarm at Orion. Orion nodded.

'As close as that?'

'They will scarcely venture closer. Not yet.'

A new urgency spurred them. Winter had struck a quick and vicious blow. From now it would be only memories, Silaire wood floating on a sea of hyacinth, the swan on the dark water, or Tubbrid where the thrush sings.

His ankle twisted in a rut and he pitched forward. Orion helped him to his feet again. He leaned heavily on the strong shoulder, found that he could still walk, but he began to doubt, for the first time he doubted. In his distress his mind flew back and he saw vividly the quiet rounded hills of another land, with their vine-terraces and dew-ponds, heard the racketting call of a pheasant as it shot up alarmed from the chalky hill, and in his desperate weariness he sobbed.

Then repentance smote him like a thunderbolt and he prayed.

'Forgive me, Lord. Thou hast ordained that here my course must be run, that in this wild and lovely place I must labour and save my soul until I lie forever under these cloudy skies. I am content. Forgive my murmurs, Lord.'

'Only a little way more,' he heard Orion's voice. He felt the massive strength of the shoulder he leaned on and the arm that kept him upright, and he was comforted, so that even when the snow began to fall again in silent whispers he did not despair. Hills, river, trees vanished. Familiar things were monsters, high and low were one, drifts hid bounds and fences. They ploughed onward. They stumbled down to a level, smoother place and had walked a hundred steps before they knew it for Clurnach road. The snow ceased to fall, the sky cleared. Where their road that was scarcely a road skirted the forest there were enormous drifts. The sloping ledges glared white with menace. They sank in it to their knees and made but slow progress.

At last they came out above their valley and saw, far down, the dark bulk of *Sancti Salvatoris*.

'Thank God,' breathed Simon, then feeling that steadying arm and remembering with regret his former impatience he added, 'And thank you, my Brother.'

From here he could make out all the walls that he knew so well. Smoke from the kitchen chimneys smudged the surrounding white, and the sickle of the dead moon hung in the sky above the octagonal tower.

Exhaustion now let his feet wander almost out of control, yet Orion was still rock-like and together they managed that last half-mile. The wheel of the year had turned full; from now we must be within, the bars of our gates must hold against flood and tempest and the stealthy snow till resurrection come to us again. Orion stopped, raised a finger; the bell was calling. They hurried past the casa and into the cloister. When they entered the church the others were already in their stalls.

Simon shrugged off his weariness, straightened his shoulders and walked determinedly to his place, defying pain, and knew that however much he loved the open sky, the fields and the woods, yet this for him was shelter and solace. The wheel had turned again and he was one more year closer to home. He hurried with joy to his prayers.

GLOSSARY

Articuli: commands and recommendations written by Stephen of Lexington during his visitation of 1228.
calefactory: a room where the monks could warm themselves at a fire before retiring.
caracole: a winding stair.
cuirass: a protective covering for the breast and back.
culver-house: dove or pigeon cote.
Deirim dán, etc: I sing a song, oh yes I sing, Any time my belly's full.
Duiske: dubh uisce, or black water, the name of the Barrow tributary which flows through Graiguenamanagh, is also the name of the Abbey.
grange: an out-farm.
Heu alas pour amour: this Norman-French ballad describes the building of the walls of New Ross.
hurdy-gurdy: used here to denote a musical instrument resembling a barrel-organ.
Iam lucis: first words of a psalm sung by the monks.
luce: pike.
mether: a wooden drinking vessel.
Nemo dat quod non habet: no-one gives what he has not.
pilibeen: plover
poitrel: armour protecting a horse's breast.
Prick-the-garter: a cheating game practised at fairs.
slype: a covered passage leading out from the cloister.
stallage: toll paid to erect a stall at a fair. This and the other rights and privileges mentioned by Brother Orion, and, rather more accurately, by Brother Simon, were at first enjoyed by the Abbey but many of them were later transferred to officers of the New Town of Graiguenamanagh.
Vallis Sancti Salvatoris: Valley of the Holy Saviour.
Via Magna: the main highway leading north and west from the Abbey. It is now known as Bohermore.